THEY'R
THEY'RE
AND
TO SAVE THE DAY!
THEY'RE THE

HEROMICE

AND THESE ARE THEIR ADVENTURES!

Geronimo Stilton

HEROMICE

REVENGE OF THE MINI-MICE

Scholastic Inc.

Published by Scholastic Inc., *Publishers since 1920*, 557 Broadway, New York, NY 10012. SCHOLASTIC and associated logos are trademarks and/or registered trademarks of Scholastic Inc.

ISBN 978-9-352-75261-4

Text by Geronimo Stilton
Original title *Mini-topi contro maxi-pantegane!*
Original design of the Heromice world by Giuseppe Facciotto and Flavio Ferron
Cover by Giuseppe Facciotto (design) and Flavio Ferron (color)
Illustrations by Luca Usai (pencils), Valeria Cairoli (inks), and Serena Gianoli and Daniele Verzini (color)
Graphics by Francesca Sirianni

Special thanks to Beth Dunfey
Translated by Julia Heim
Interior design by Kevin Callahan/BNGO Books

First printing 2018

Reprinted by Scholastic India Pvt. Ltd., 2018 (Twice), 2019

Printed in India by Repro India Ltd.

When darkness falls over Muskrat City, the Sewer Rats slither into the alleys to cause chaos aboveground. But the citizens of Muskrat City know that there are mysterious figures watching over them, ready to fight evil at all costs.

They are strong, they are invincible, they are fearless — well, almost . . .

They are the Heromice!

MEET THE HEROMICE!

GERONIMO SUPERSTILTON

The strongest hero in Muskrat City . . . but he still must learn how to control his powers!

SWIFTPAWS

Geronimo Superstilton's partner in crimefighting; he can transform his supersuit into anything.

LADY WONDERWHISKERS

A mysterious mouse with special powers; she always seems to be in the right place at the right time.

TESS TECHNOPAWS

A cook and scientist who assists the Heromice with every mission.

ELECTRON AND PROTON

Supersmart mouselets who help the Heromice; they create and operate sophisticated technological gadgets.

AND THE SEWER RATS!

TONY SLUDGE

The undisputed leader of the Sewer Rats; known for being tough and mean.

TERESA SLUDGE

Tony's wife; makes the important decisions for their family.

ELENA SLUDGE

Tony and Teresa's teenage daughter; has a real weakness for rat metal music.

SLICKFUR

Sludge's right-hand mouse; the true (and only) brains behind the Sewer Rats.

ONE, TWO, AND THREE

Bodyguards who act as Sludge's henchmice; they are big, buff, and brainless.

The Quest for Clean Laundry

It was a beautiful spring morning, and I woke up bright and early. You see, I had something very urgent to do: my laundry!

I know it doesn't sound that urgent. But I had run out of clean shirts, clean pants, clean sweaters, and . . . *squeak*! I didn't even have a clean robe or pajamas to put on.

It was vital that I wash my clothes right away, but . . . guess what? My washing machine was **broken**!

Oh, excuse me, I almost forgot to introduce myself!

My name is Stilton, *Geronimo Stilton*,

and I run *The Rodent's Gazette*, the most famouse **NEWSPAPER** on Mouse Island.

As I was saying, my washing machine broke on the day I had absolutely zero clean clothes. And when the machine broke, it **flooded** the entire basement!

I immediately called Shorty Circuit, the most savvy and skilled repairmouse in New Mouse City. I dialed Shorty's number.

Riiiiing . . . riiiiing . . . riiiiing . . .

BEEP!

"This is Shorty Circuit's voicemail. I'm out on a job, and I have **ANOTHER** *job right after that, and then* **ANOTHER ONE** *right after that. You see, I'm super busy! But leave a message and I'll call you back if I get around to it . . ."*

Click!

Oh no! **Now what?!**

At that moment, I spotted a flyer poking out of my mailbox.

> TIRED OF WRINKLED CLOTHES AND FADED COLORS?
>
> TIRED OF USING THE WRONG CYCLE AND TURNING ALL YOUR SOCKS PINK?
>
> THEN COME TO THE WASH-O-MATIC, THE MOST TECHNOLOGICALLY ADVANCED LAUNDROMAT IN NEW MOUSE CITY!

WHAT GOOD LUCK! The ad seemed designed just for absentminded rodents like me.

I shoved my clothes into two overflowing bags and *HURRIED* over to the Wash-o-matic. Inside were dozens of washing machines covered with blinking lights and flashing **buttons**. Customers scurried between the washers and the cheese-scented detergent dispensers.

SWEET SOAPSUDS! What a busy place! I scampered up to an empty washing machine and stuffed my clothes inside. A recorded squeak said:

"Please insert a coin and press the START button."

So I slid a coin in, pressed a random button, and . . . glub! A stream of water hit me straight in the snout!

"Maybe it's this button . . ." I muttered.

Whoops! Steam poured from the machine, surrounding

my snout in a cloud of vapor!

I tried again. "Umm . . . maybe it's this one?"

"You have selected the super-speedy spin-cycle mode!" the prerecorded squeak announced.

"Noooooo! That's not what I want!" I cried.

At that moment, my phone began to ring.

RIIING!
RIIING!!
RIIING!!!

"Hello, Shorty Circuit, is that you?" I asked HOPEFULLY.

"Shorty Circuit? Who in the name of soft cheese is Shorty Circuit?" a squeak answered. “It’s me, Swiftpaws, your favorite superpartner!”

“Oh, Swiftpaws, hey, how are you?” I muttered.

“I’m just cheesy!” he replied. “But I need my hero partner on the double. So fly on over to Muskrat City RIGHT AWAY! This city needs the Heromice!”

“Can’t you tell me what’s going on first?” I protested.

“Get your tail in gear, Geronimo!” he squeaked. “This isn’t an emergency, it’s a SUPER-EMERGENCY!” Then he hung up.

I sighed. I had to answer the call. I couldn’t bear to let down my fellow Heromice.

Quiet as a mouse, I left the Wash-o-matic (and my laundry) and slipped down a nearby alley.

Then I pulled the **Superpen** out of my pocket, pressed the secret button, and . . .

BZZZZT!

A ray of green light surrounded me from the ends of my whiskers to the tip of my tail. Instantly, I was **transformed** into Superstilton!

Now came my least favorite part of being a Heromouse. It was time to take to the skies. I hate flying—you see, I am a true scaredy-mouse—but I had no choice. My friends needed me! So I **leaped** into the air and sped over the New Mouse City skyline.

THREAT AT RATCASH RESERVE

The trip was smooth. In a flash, I'd arrived in **MUSKRAT CITY**. I zoomed toward my ultimate destination, Heromice Headquarters, at supersonic speeds.

I was *gliding* toward a park nearby when suddenly . . .

Splat!

I smashed right into a kite! Yee-ouch!

The kite's tail wrapped around my super-cape, and I lost control.

"**HEEELLLP!**" I shouted.

I was hurtling down, down, down toward the ground. I tumbled snout over tail to the garden outside Heromice Headquarters.

And then . . .

Crash! I LANDED right in front of Swiftpaws! *Flaming fondue*, what an embarrassing entrance.

"Superstilton, that was super quick!" he greeted me. "Great job, hero partner!"

"*Ouchie,*" I muttered. "Uh, thanks. So, here I am. Now can you please tell me what the big emergency is?"

"CRISPY CHEESE CHUNKS, I didn't mention it?" Swiftpaws asked. "The Sewer Rats are about to strike."

"Really?" I asked.

TESS, the Heromice's fabumouse inventor and cook, scurried over to us.

Her assistants, Proton and ELECTRON, were right behind her.

"We don't know what Tony's plan is yet," Tess said. "But he seems to have a **big trick** up his tail."

Proton nodded. "That cheesebrain flew his plane over Muskrat City . . ."

". . . and he tossed out a bunch of flyers!" Electron concluded.

Swiftpaws pawed me a piece of paper.

"Did I read that right?" I exclaimed in surprise. "Tony is planning to strike **RatCash Reserve**?!" It was the enormouse fort where the city stored all its gold.

Tess nodded. "Yes, Tony wants to steal the city's GOLD reserves."

"But . . . but . . . that place is superprotected, SUPERARMORED, and under SUPER-DUPER SURVEILLANCE!"

Dear citizens of Muskrat City,

Today at noon, I will strike RatCash Reserve! I will snatch all of Muskrat City's gold. And then I will become the supreme ruler of the city! Ha, ha, ha!

Yours in crime,
Tony Sludge

"Yet Tony is confident he can do it," Tess commented thoughtfully.

"**Super Swiss cheese**, there's no time to lose!" Swiftpaws said. "It's already eleven o'clock. Are you ready, my dear Superstilton? Because **WE NEED TO SHAKE A TAIL**!

"Supersuit: Flying scooter mode!"

In a flash, he had transformed into a supersleek scooter.

Tess, Proton, and Electron climbed on, but when I tried to join them, Swiftpaws stopped me. "We're all full, superpartner! You can hold on to the luggage rack. Hee, hee, hee!"

"Whaaaat?!" I protested. "The luggage rack?! B-but that's not safe . . ."

But Swiftpaws had already revved his engines, and the super-scooter roared to life. I had no choice but to reach out and grab on!

When we arrived at RatCash Reserve, we found a line of police surrounding the fort.

"TONY will never manage to sneak into the underground vault," thundered the police commissioner, REX RATFORD. "If he tries, he'll get a one-way ticket to Mousekatraz prison."

"We must be ready!" said Swiftpaws.

"Well put, Swiftpaws!" a **PLUCKY** squeak rang out from behind us. "What do you say, Heromice? Shall we head inside?"

I turned around to see who had spoken. **Great chunks of cheddar**, there she was! It was **Lady Wonderwhiskers**, of course! She is the most captivating defender of justice.

Squeak! My heart has a spot as soft as Brie when it comes to that spectacular Heromouse.

She is the rodent of my dreams!

The fort is surrounded . . .
Let's get inside!
Lady Wonderwhiskers!

Welcome to RatCash Reserve!

The head of RatCash Reserve, Wallace Watchrat, led us inside the fort. Great gobs of Gorgonzola, the tunnels below RatCash Reserve had more twists and turns than a lab rat's ***MAZE***! There were dozens and dozens of cameras, supersensitive alarms, and sophisticated booby traps hidden behind every **corner**.

To reach the top-secret vault, we needed to pass through the following:

→ a **PRESSURE-SENSITIVE ALARM** hidden in the ground (one wrong step would

drop you through a trapdoor into a veeeery dark tunnel!);

- an **intricate network of lasers** (to cross it, we had to perform some serious acrobatic moves!);
- and **a gazillion guards** (who were ready to jump into action at a moment's notice).

"Here we are," Mr. Watchrat said, pointing

to a shatterproof glass window into the vault.

"Super Swiss slices!" Swiftpaws exclaimed in amazement. "But that's . . .

". . . a room full of GOLD BARS!" I gasped, stunned.

"I remember this vault quite well," Tess commented. "Years ago, I helped the architect who designed it."

"Really?!" Proton and Electron exclaimed, gazing at their boss in admiration.

"Yes, it's true," Tess said with a SMILE. "And I can confirm it's the safest place in Muskrat City. This glass can stand up to any kind of attack:

piercing lasers,

superpowered drills, and

even the most advanced explosives!

"There is no material in existence that can even SCRATCH it! Believe me, we've got nothing to worry about."

Mr. Watchrat nodded. "The same is true for the walls inside the safe. They are solid steel and absolutely Drillmobile-proof."

"So how does Tony think he can get in there and NAB the gold bars?" I wondered.

Swiftpaws stuck his snout in the air and sniffed. "Do you smell that?" he asked.

We all shook our snouts.

"It's a trap!" Swiftpaws explained. "Tony is going to try to pull the cheesecloth over our EYES. We must stay alert!"

"Heromice, it's almost noon," Commissioner Ratford exclaimed, pointing to a clock on the wall. "Tony could strike any moment now."

We all held our breath.

Ticktock . . . ticktock . . .

Ratford paced back and forth.

Ticktock . . . ticktock . . .

Swiftpaws began to twirl his whiskers.

Ticktock . . . ticktock . . .

Lady Wonderwhiskers kept her eyes glued to the bars of gold on the other side of the glass.

Ticktock . . . ticktock . . .

There was no sound and no movement. That minute was so looooong, it seemed to stretch on forever!

Finally, Swiftpaws let out a *sigh* of relief. "It's a minute past noon. Nothing happened!"

"Wait!" Lady Wonderwhiskers exclaimed. "Look down there!"

She was pointing to a **strange** object inside the safe on the other side of the glass.

"**CHEWY CHEDDAR CHUNKS**, what is *that*?" Tess asked in disbelief.

"There's an insect inside my safe!" Mr. Watchrat moaned.

"That's no insect . . ." Swiftpaws began.

"No?" I asked. "Then what is it?"

"It's a tiny **Tony Sludge**!" Lady Wonderwhiskers exclaimed.

Slickfur's Shrink Ray

Swiftpaws and I pressed our snouts against the glass to get a better look. **For the love of cheese**, it really was a tiny Tony Sludge, the leader of the Sewer Rats! What was he doing in there? And how did he get **so small**?

At that moment . . .

BEEP! BEEP! BEEP!

Swiftpaws's wrist communicator began to vibrate.

"Hello? Hello?" he answered it.

The reply? Tony's **WICKED** laugh!

"**Ha, ha, ha!** Greetings, you cheesy chumps!" came the high-pitched squeak of the leader of the SEWER RATS. "Here I am, just two pawsteps away from you! So, did you like my little trick?"

"You two-bit SEWER RAT!" Swiftpaws exclaimed. "Is that really you? What happened? Why are you so small?"

"It's simple," Tiny Tony continued. "I used Slickfur's brand-new invention, the Supershrink Ray! Want to see how it works? Then pay attention!"

He pulled out a strange gadget that looked like a remote control. He pointed it at the gold, and . . .

ZAAAPP!!!

The gold bars began to get **smaller** . . . **and smaller** . . . **and smaller still** . . .

Soon they'd become nothing more than

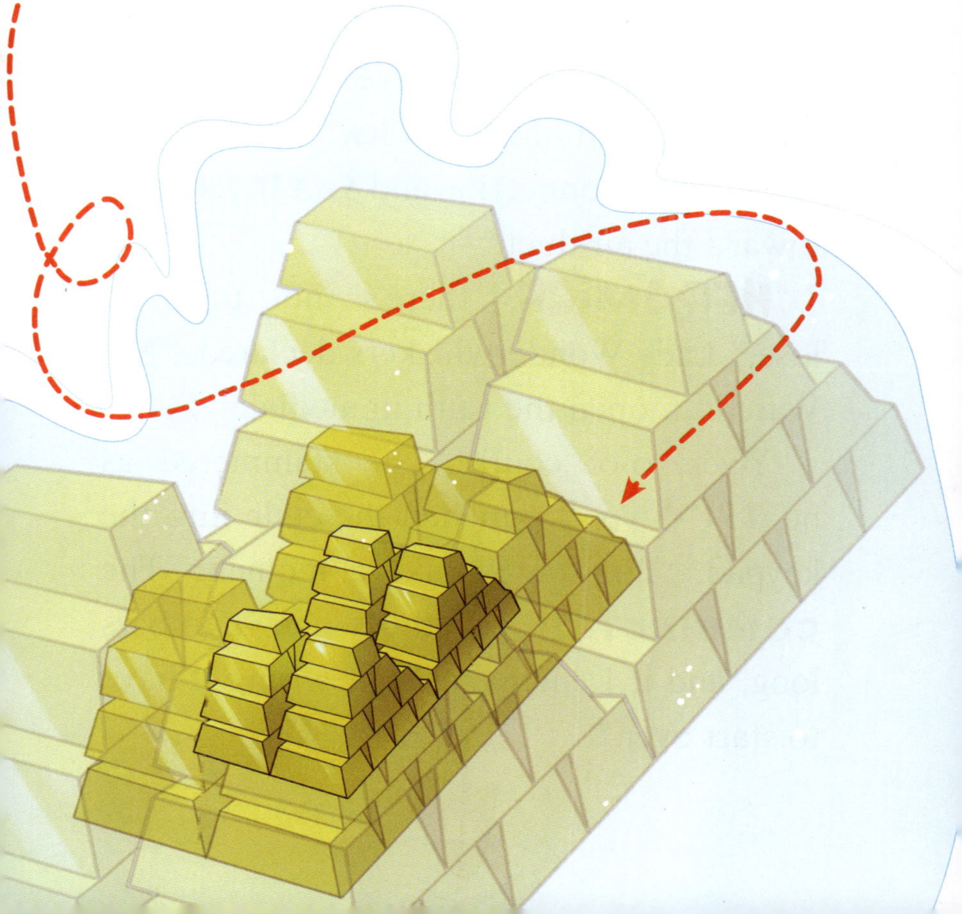

a pile of sparkly crumbs! Tony scurried to sweep them up, tucking them safely in his pocket.

"Microscopic mozzarella!" Swiftpaws exclaimed. "HOW IS THAT POSSIBLE?"

"Now, if you'll excuse me, Heromice," Tiny Tony sneered. "I have some pressing business out in Muskrat City."

He cut the connection and scampered toward the air duct.

"HEROMICE, there's no time to lose," Lady Wonderwhiskers declared. "Mr. Watchrat, open the vault immediately!"

"Y-yes, o-of course," he stammered as he nervously punched the code into the keypad. "But it will take a moment. The COMBINATION is thirty-one numbers long, and if I enter one digit wrong, I have to start over."

"Come on, move those paws!" Swiftpaws urged. "Tony is getting away!"

But Swiftpaws's urging just gave Mr. Watchrat the jitters.

Ticktock . . .

Ticktock . . . ticktock . . .

Finally, the glass door slid open.

Lady Wonderwhiskers and Swiftpaws leaped inside the vault, dragging me along with them. **How do I get myself into these crazy messes?!**

Swiftpaws **bounded** toward Tony and loomed over him threateningly.

"Stop right there, Tony! SURRENDER!"

"Now, that doesn't seem like a fair fight, does it?" Tony snickered. "You're big and I'm tiny. But I can fix that!" He pointed the shrink ray at us and pressed the power button.

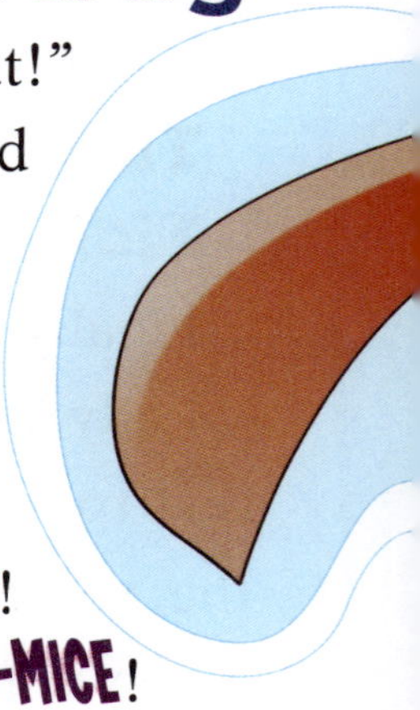

A ray hit us full on!

ZAAAAPPPP!!!

Oh no! We were getting smaller!

Mighty mozzarella, we were MINI-MICE!

Tony took advantage of our confusion and slipped away.

"Look!" Lady Wonderwhiskers yelled. "Tony went

down that air duct!"

"He's ***escaping***!" Swiftpaws exclaimed.

"We have to **Stop** him! **Mini Heromice in action!**"

As we scurried through the duct, we heard **TESS** call after us.

"Good luck, Heromice!" she squeaked. "Muskrat City is with you. But watch your tails! And meet me back at headquarters when you've caught Tony."

Catch Me If You Can!

We ***HURRIED*** after the leader of the Sewer Rats. But the air duct was **darker** than the inside of a cat's mouth! It was so **DARK** you couldn't tell a cat from a rat.

"**Catch me if you can, Heromice!**" Tony taunted.

We scurried after him. We couldn't let him get away with all that GOLD! We headed farther and farther underground.

"I think he went that way," Lady Wonderwhiskers said, pointing to a tunnel on the right.

We turned to the RIGHT, then to the left. Then we went UP, then we went down, until . . .

"Yuck!" I cried, covering my nose. "What a stench!"

Lady Wonderwhiskers nodded grimly. "We've entered the sewer system."

And we were so small that the trickle of dirty water next to us seemed like a RAGING RIVER of sludge!

Then we heard pawsteps coming toward us.

"Look! There's someone there!" Lady

Wonderwhiskers exclaimed.

We were about to flee when an enormouse *shadow* loomed over us.

"Cheese and crackers, what is it?" Swiftpaws asked in alarm.

The shadow turned the corner and . . . **CHEWY CHEDDAR CHUNKS**!

It was a giant Slickfur, Tony Sludge's wicked assistant!

Faster than a mousetrap spring, **Slickfur** pounced on us.

CLANG!!!

Before we could move a mouscle, he'd trapped us under a **glass jar**!

"I got 'em!" he yelled to his boss. "The Heromice are truly **trapped** this time!"

Tony stepped out of the darkness, cackling triumphantly. Then he turned the shrink ray on himself, and . . .

ZAAAAPPP!!!

Instantly, he was his normal size again!

"**Ha, ha, ha!** This time I've done it, you meddling mouselings," he rejoiced. "I've finally defeated the Heromice!"

"**We'll be the judges of that, Tony!**" I squeaked, summoning all the courage I could muster.

"**Oh, really?** Just who's left to stop me?" Tony asked. "It's certainly not a job for teensy-tiny mini-mice like you three!"

Tony signaled to Slickfur, and in a flash, his sidekick **tied up** Swiftpaws, Lady

Wonderwhiskers, and me like three mini cheeses.

The leader of the Sewer Rats picked up a *page* from the newspaper and began folding it, whistling cheerfully.

WHAT WAS HE UP TO NOW?

"Here we go." He CHORTLED. "I hope none of you get seasick, because you're

about to take a **little cruise**. Anchors aweigh!"

"Wait! Stop!" Lady Wonderwhiskers protested. "Turn us back to our normal size and fight us honestly, like real mice!"

"So **SORRY**, but I've never been the **honest** type." Tony snickered. "And I have other things to do!

"I need to find a place to hide all this ***gold***! Have a nice trip, mini Goody Two-paws. **HA, HA, HA!**"

Then he put down the little boat he'd made out of newspaper, placed us inside it, and dropped it into a trickle of sewer sludge. A moment later, the current began pulling us away!

Oh no . . . **now what**?!

A NOT-SO-NICE CRUISE

The boat **swayed** dangerously as we floated through the stinky sewer water. My whiskers trembled with **terror**!

"Let's not lose our snouts," Lady Wonderwhiskers said calmly. "First we need to get out of these **ROPES**."

"I have an idea," Swiftpaws said quickly. **"Supersuit: Scissor mode!"**

In a flash my hero partner transformed

into a pair of scissors and began to CUT us free.

"Smart thinking, Swiftpaws!" Lady Wonderwhiskers squeaked.

"H-hey, Heromice . . ." I stammered.

"Just a sec, Superstilton, you're next," Swiftpaws replied.

"No, it's not that . . . we have another PROBLEM!" I exclaimed. "Look down there!"

My two superpartners turned and looked ahead of us.

"Mighty mozzarella! We're about to hit the RAPIDS!" Swiftpaws gasped. "Hurry! Let's move those paws!" He quickly cut through our ropes.

Meanwhile, the current was getting stronger and stronger and more and more intense.

"**HANG ON TIGHT!**" Lady Wonderwhiskers yelled as she grabbed the edge of the newspaper boat. A moment later . . .

Whoooooosshhh!

The little boat **reared** upward, flipped, and landed on the crest of a **WAVE**.

PHEW!

But the danger wasn't over yet.

There was an enormouse can floating straight for us!

"Supersuit: Chainsaw mode!"

Swiftpaws transformed into a yellow chainsaw and cut the can in two. The two halves separated, **FILLED** with water, and sank. Saved by a whisker!

"That was a **close** call," I said, sighing in relief.

But just then, I heard a **roar**.

"W-what in the name of cheese was that?" I stammered.

"It sounds like a *waterfall*!" Swiftpaws shouted.

The current kept dragging us along and the boat began to tilt.

"**FLOATING CHEESE BALLS!**" I exclaimed.

Then I closed my **eyes**, preparing for the **WORST**.

But then I bumped against something

SOFT and **bulky**, so I grabbed it and squeezed it as hard as I could.

When I opened my eyes, my snout dropped. It really *was* a floating ball of **cheese**! My cheesy superpowers had summoned a ton of flying, floating cheese balls!

We each grabbed on to a ball. Using them as buoys, we **paddled** toward the water's edge.

"Grab my paw, Lady Wonderwhiskers," I exclaimed, helping my fellow Heromouse out of the water.

"Thanks, Superstilton," she replied. "What's our next move?"

"I suggest we ask Tess for ***HELP***," Swiftpaws replied. "Are we ready to go back to headquarters?"

He **pointed** at the ceiling. Far above our snouts, there was a sewer hole leading to the street. We **GAZED** up at it for a moment.

Swiftpaws winked at us. Then he grabbed

Lady Wonderwhiskers and me by the paws and activated his supersuit's **supersonic boots**. We zoomed up toward the street.

"Heromice in action!" Swiftpaws exclaimed. "We're heading back to **base**!"

BLOCKED BY BUTTERFLIES!

We crawled out of the sewer hole and found ourselves smack in the middle of Muskrat City. *Fresh air at last!*

"Mini muenster chunks!" Swiftpaws commented. "We're so tiny, everything else is **ENORMOUSE**."

My superpartner was right — the cars seemed as **TALL** as houses and the houses as **TALL** as mountains! The pawsteps of the rodents scurrying down the street made the ground shake like a wheel of **Brie**.

"Let's get moving before somebody steps on us and turns us into micemeat," said Lady Wonderwhiskers.

Slimy Swiss!
Huh?!
Everything is enormouse!

She led us across the busy street and into the PARK.

"This place is so familiar," I said.

"Of course it is. This is the park that's across the street from Heromice Headquarters!" Lady Wonderwhiskers explained. "We're almost there."

Lady Wonderwhiskers was right: We weren't far. But, unfortunately, a PUDDLE stood between us and our destination. It seemed as deep and wide as a lake.

"Cheese niblets!" I said with a sigh. "How can we scamper across this puddle when we're so puny?"

"Who said we need to SCAMPER across it? We'll FLY!" Swiftpaws replied. Then he transformed into a yellow and orange biplane.

"But I hate heights!" I protested.

"Swiftpaws, you know what a 'fraidy mouse I am."

Lady Wonderwhiskers, on the other paw, absolutely loved to fly. She reached out to help me CLIMB aboard.

Holey cheese, how could I refuse?!

"Now I understand how a fly must feel," I remarked as we whizzed between BRANCHES.

"Uh-huh," Swiftpaws muttered as we flew. "Squeaking of insects, that bird has his eye on us. I'm pretty sure he's decided to make us his lunch!"

"WHAAAAAT?!" I exclaimed.

I turned around and . . . **squeeeak**! A bird was pointing its open beak right at us.

"Flying fish sticks, let's get out of here!" Swiftpaws shrieked. "Otherwise we're going to become bird feed!"

SWWWWWOOSH!

We glided between the branches of the trees and **ZIGZAGGED** over leaves, dodging the bird.

We were super-fast! Faster than a gerbil on a wheel! Faster than the mouse who ran up the clock! Even faster than the scent of melting cheese on a breeze!

But just when we thought we were safe, two **giant** butterflies blocked our escape path.

SWWWWISH!

At the last minute, Swiftpaws did a **super-duper triple flip** past the butterflies, and we escaped. Phew!

"**SEE?!**" Swiftpaws said triumphantly. "We're fine!"

"Whoa! Careful!" Lady Wonderwhiskers cried out. "We're about to hit a—"

SPLAT!

Too late. We had smacked right into a billboard!

We bounced off it like a ping-pong ball and fell down, down, down . . .

A moment before we hit the ground, we landed on something soft and cushiony.

BOING! BOING! BOING!

"Ouch, ouch, ouchie!" my hero partner exclaimed. "Why is there a net here?"

"It's not a net," Lady Wonderwhiskers responded. "It's a spiderweb!"

"Eeeeek!" I yelled. I was staring right at an ENORMOUSE spider!

Terror made my tail go as STIFF as a petrified cheese stick. I scrambled around, trying to untangle myself from the web's sticky strings.

But I just got even more snarled up!

Watch out!
It's a spider!
Yikes!

WHAT A CAT-ASTROPHE!

"I'll handle this," Lady Wonderwhiskers declared. She pulled a super high-tech **nail file** out of her pocket.

"This is no time to file your pawnails, Lady Wonderwhiskers," Swiftpaws said with a scowl.

"Don't you worry your pretty little snout, **Swiftpaws**!" she replied with a wink.

A moment later . . . *ziiippp!*

The nail file cut through the spiderweb, and we ***DASHED*** away.

"Super Swiss slices!" Swiftpaws shouted. "Great work, Lady Wonderwhiskers!"

A STICKY TRAP

To avoid other dangerous insect encounters, we decided to continue on paw. But we were so tiny that the park felt like an overgrown jungle! The LEAVES were as big as bed sheets, the FLOWERS seemed like giant chandeliers, and the BLADES OF GRASS were as tall as lampposts.

"Watch where you put your **paws**," Lady Wonderwhiskers warned us.

Ahhh, Lady Wonderwhiskers . . .

What a dazzling smile,
what a sweet squeak,
what wonderful whiskers!

The sight of her made me melt like **string cheese** in the sun. Just scampering next to

Let's go on paw!
Uh, okay . . .
Be careful!

her made my heart beat faster than a snare drum.

Great Gouda, I was thinking dreamily of Lady Wonderwhiskers when—

SQUISH!

"Superstilton!" Swiftpaws **scolded** me. "Get your snout out of the clouds and watch where you're going!"

SQUEAK! I'd been so lost in thought that I'd stepped in a puddle of sticky pink goo. Now my paws were stuck!

"It's the newest flavor of chewing gum, strawberry Brie!" Lady Wonderwhiskers said, sniffing the puddle.

"Some lazymouse must have tossed it on the ground instead of in the garbage can," I said with a sigh.

Swiftpaws just shook his snout.

"Ick!" he squeaked. "Why is it so hard for

some rodents to put their gum in the trash?" Swiftpaws wondered.

I was trying to extract my paws when . . .

BOOM!

BOOM!!

BOOM!!!

The ground began to tremble like a bowl of fondue!

"Oh no!" I squeaked, my whiskers quivering in fright. "What now?!"

Someone was jogging down the path, and he was heading right toward us!

"COME ON, WE'VE GOT TO HAUL TAIL!"

Swiftpaws exclaimed. "We don't want to be crushed under his paws!"

"Someone help me!" I cried. "I'm still

stuck in this chewing gum!"

Lady Wonderwhiskers grabbed my paws and began to PULL and PULL.

BOOM!

BOOM!!

BOOM!!!

The rodent was getting closer and closer.

The gum stretched like a RUBBER BAND until finally . . .

BOOOOOING!

There was a loud snap. For a moment, I thought I was free. But then I bounced back and ended up exactly where I'd started!

Meanwhile, the rodent runner was getting closer and closer.

BOOM! BOOM!!! BOOM!!

"Heeeelp!" I exclaimed.

"Supersuit: Spatula mode!" Swiftpaws cried.

My *superpartner* transformed into a giant spatula and scraped the chewing gum off the path. I managed to wriggle away seconds before I became Heromouse hash!

PHEW!

I scraped the last bits of gum off my boots and cape. Then the three of us hurried into headquarters.

For once, being superting worked to our advantage. We slipped behind a vent grate and scurried straight into the living room.

"I wonder if Tess, Proton, and Electron are back yet," Lady Wonderwhiskers said.

"Oh, I'm sure they've returned by now. It's been hours since they told us to meet them here," I replied.

At that moment, Proton appeared at the door.

"Yoo-hoooo!"

Swiftpaws exclaimed, waving his paws. "We're here!"

But we were so small and our squeaks were so **SOFT** that Proton couldn't hear us. And naturally, he couldn't **see** us either.

Watch Your Paws, Superstilton!

Proton was squeaking on the phone.

"ELECTRON, have you heard from the Heromice?" he asked. "I can't seem to get through to them! My WRIST COMMUNICATOR has lost their signal."

"We're down here!" we squeaked, waving our paws to get his attention.

"Wait a minute," he said, pricking up his ears. "I think I hear something . . ."

"Yoo-hoo! It's us!" Swiftpaws yelled. "Look down!"

"Maybe there's SOMEONE at the door," Proton said. He took a big step toward us.

Have you heard anything?
Yoo-hoo!
Look down!
Stop!

"STOP!" I yelled as loud as I could. But he still didn't hear us. "GREAT GOUDA! He's going to flatten us! He'll make us into micemeat! He'll completely crush us!"

"Quick, do something, Superstilton!" Lady Wonderwhiskers cried out.

"Fly to him and tickle his paw!" Swiftpaws shouted. "He'll have to look down, and then he'll see us."

"Fly?!" I squeaked. "But I HATE flying! I'm afraid of heights!"

"You can do it, Superstilton!" Lady Wonderwhiskers encouraged me.

Holey cheese, I couldn't disappoint the rodent of my dreams! So I gathered all my courage and . . .

Whoooooosh!

I took off!

I did a **SUPERSPIN** around Proton's paws and began to tickle him. **But nothing happened!**

So I flew farther up, grabbed a corner of his sweatshirt, and yanked it. *But still nothing!*

"Protoooooon, I'm right here!" I yelled at the top of my lungs.

But he still didn't **notice** me. How was I going to get his attention?

I **tried** again, flying higher and higher until I was hovering right in front of his eyes.

"**Hey, what's that?**" Proton exclaimed. "Just a minute! Superstilton? Is that you?!"

"Yep, it's me!" I exclaimed. "And Swiftpaws and Lady Wonderwhiskers are right down there."

"There you are, finally!" our friend rejoiced. "Electron and I have been so **worried** about you."

He kneeled down and scooped up my mini partners and me in his paws. Then he brought us into the kitchen to see Tess. Proton placed us carefully on the kitchen table and scurried down to the **LABORATORY** to call Electron, who returned to headquarters a few minutes later.

Our resident **GENIUS** scientist-cook peered at us through a magnifying glass.

"*Particles and pastries*, I knew you'd get here sooner or later!" Tess smiled. "I'm trying to find a way to **reverse** the effects of the shrink ray."

"And have you figured it out yet?" I asked eagerly.

"**Not yet**," Tess admitted. "I must admit that **SLICKFUR'S** invention is groovier than Gorgonzola."

"But have no fear, Heromice!" Proton said. "There has to be a **SOLUTION**."

At that moment, his paw bumped into a pepper grinder that stood next to

us. The grinder shook, swayed, and tipped over, sending a CLOUD of pepper into the air. Swiftpaws, Lady Wonderwhiskers, and I began coughing.

"Watch where you put your paws, Proton," Electron scolded him.

"Oops . . . sorry!" he said, blushing redder than a cheese rind.

"Don't worry about it," said Swiftpaws. "Look at Superstilton. He's clumsier than a gopher in a garbage can. He's always knocking into things. AH . . . AH . . . ACHOO!"

My superpartner sneezed, and a moment later . . .

ZAAAM!

He started growing. In a flash, he'd returned to his normal size!

Gooey globs of Gouda . . . *what had just happened*?

Oooh!
Look out . . .
Whoa!
What happened?
Get out of the way!

THE FIX-IT-ALL SNEEZE

We all **STARED** at Swiftpaws, our snouts hanging open.

"Well, what are you staring at?" he demanded. "Haven't you ever seen a Heromouse **sneeze**?"

"Take a good look at yourself, Swiftpaws!" Electron exclaimed, stunned.

"Huh?" he said. "**THUNDERING CATTAILS**, I've gone back to my normal size!" he cried. "How is that possible?!"

"Even a simple sneeze can alter your **molecular** balance," Tess explained. "It must have reversed the effects of the shrink ray."

Before she could finish squeaking, Swiftpaws started throwing pawfuls of pepper into the air.

"Super Swiss slices!" he squeaked. "We need more sneezes. Come on, **pepper** all around! Who's next?"

Lady Wonderwhiskers took a handful of pepper and blew on it. A gray cloud formed around her snout, and she took a deep breath.

"Achoo!"

she sneezed.

With one big **SNEEZE**, she popped back to her full size.

"We did it!"

Proton CHEERED. "This is the solution we've been looking for! We've figured out how to reverse the effects of Slickfur's shrink ray."

"It's your turn, Superstilton," Lady Wonderwhiskers declared.

"Umm . . . are we totally sure this will work?" I asked.

"Yes!" she replied confidently. "Now come on."

So I grabbed a pawful of pepper and rubbed it into my snout.

My nose tickled, my eyes watered, my throat burned, but . . . NO SNEEZES!

"I'll handle this, hero partner!" Swiftpaws exclaimed, picking up a feather. "A little tickle is what you need!"

Before I could protest, Swiftpaws began to wave the feather under my whiskers.

But that didn't work, either!

"Umm . . . let's try this," my superpartner said.

He began to WAVE the feather around my snout, then again under my nose, then under my armpits.

"HA, HA, HA! THAT'S ENOUGH! HEE, HEE, HEE! STOP IT! HO, HO, HO! LEAVE ME ALONE!"

But once again, nothing happened.

"Cheese puffs, there must be a way to

make you sneeze," said Tess, shaking her snout.

She began rummaging through the kitchen cupboards.

We tried:

1 an entire jar of SNEEZING POWDER (my eyes watered, but no sneezing!);

2 two bottles of sniffle formula (my mouth burned, but no sneezing!);

3 a vial of tickle crystals (my fur itched, but I didn't sneeze once!).

After a while, we gave up. **We'd tried**

everything we could think of!

"Crusty cheddar chunks!" Tess exclaimed. "This is a real **PROBLEM**."

"Don't get your paws in a pickle, Superstilton!" Swiftpaws encouraged me. "We've just got to try a little harder."

"**Try harder?!**" I exclaimed. "We've tried everything! I just can't sneeze on command."

As I turned away from him, I tripped on the handle of a teaspoon.

SQUEAK!

I stumbled across the table and TUMBLED to the ground, coming to a stop next to the broom and dustpan.

"You all right, Superstilton?" Proton asked.

"Ouch, ouch, ouchie, that hurt!" I whined.

Suddenly, a speck of dust flew up my nose. At once, my whiskers began to quiver . . .

"Maybe . . . sniff . . ." I muttered.

My eyes began to water.

"I'm finally about to . . . sniff, sniff . . ."

My whiskers began to feel ticklish.

"I feel like I could . . . sniff, sniff, sniff . . .

"Aaaachoooooo!"

CHEESECAKE, I'd finally managed to sneeze! Instantly, I returned to my normal size.

"Yay! Good job, Superstilton," Lady Wonderwhiskers said warmly. "I KNEW you could do it."

"Now the day is saved!" Swiftpaws exclaimed, patting me on the tail.

"Oh, I wouldn't say that," I replied. "Tony Sludge still has all the GOLD from RatCash Reserve, remember?"

"I have something that can help," Tess said with a smile, pulling a strange object out of her apron pocket. "Introducing the Gold-o-Meter! If there's gold nearby, the needle on this gadget will point in the right direction."

"Rancid rat hairs, that's amazing, Tess!" Swiftpaws rejoiced. "Finding those two-

bit sewer rats will be easier than taking a cheese pop from a mouseling. What do you say, **Heromice**?"

"I say let's do it!" exclaimed Lady Wonderwhiskers. "What are we waiting for?

HEROMICE IN ACTION!"

Don't Lose the Gold-o-Meter!

Ten minutes later, we were back in the Muskrat City sewers. But at least this time we were full-sized.

"So what does the Gold-o-Meter say?" Swiftpaws asked.

"The needle is **pointing** this way," Lady Wonderwhiskers said, indicating a narrow tunnel to our right.

We scurried down the tunnel. Once again we turned **right** and then **left**. Then we climbed four flights of stairs, and then we went **down** and **down** and **down**. Then we climbed back **up** and **up** and **up**.

"Um, are we sure this **gizmo** actually

works?" Swiftpaws complained. "We've already passed this spot a few times."

"Look!" Lady Wonderwhiskers whispered, pointing down a SUPERNARROW tunnel.

We took a few pawsteps down the tunnel.

Holey hunks of Havarti!

In front of us lay a giant underground room. There were lights hanging haphazardly from the ceiling, illuminating a mountain of sparkly GOLD BARS! And that wasn't all . . .

"Tony Sludge is here!" I exclaimed.

"So is SLICKFUR!" Swiftpaws said. "And ONE, TWO, and THREE!"

Half of Tony's henchmice were moving the gold bars, and the other HALF were counting them. They were so busy cackling

Grunt . . .
Ugh . . . this is heavy!
Come on, you can do it!
Puff! Pant!

over their loot, they didn't even notice us.

"I'm a **genius**!" Tony snickered. "No one will think of looking for the **RatCash Reserve** gold in this abandoned subway station.

"Ha, ha, ha!"

"Umm, Boss . . ." **ONE** muttered. "Couldn't we store the loot closer to Rottington?"

"Are you kidding?!" Tony thundered. "If my beloved wife and my sweet daughter discovered we'd stolen all this treasure, they'd make me share it with **them**! But I need it all for me, for my own projects." He picked up one of the **GOLD BARS** and clutched it to his chest.

"And what would these projects be, Boss?" **ONE** asked.

"Oh, you know," said Tony, waving one paw. "I'll buy all of **MUSKRAT CITY**!

Then I'll make a new Drillmobile— one that's studded with DIAMONDS!

"Then I'll purchase a lifetime supply of **aged cheddar chunks**!"

"What about us, Boss?" TWO asked hopefully. "Can we buy a little something, too?"

"We shall see, we shall see," Tony said dismissively. "Now get back to work! The sooner we finish this, the sooner we can CONQUER the city."

"You're not going to conquer anything!" Lady Wonderwhiskers said, leaping out from her hiding spot. Swiftpaws and I followed.

"You again!" Tony cried. "What are you doing here, you pesky Heromice?"

"And how did you get back to normal size?" Slickfur squeaked in shock.

"We're **supersmart**, you super-scoundrel," Lady Wonderwhiskers replied. "Now put up your paws!"

"*That's right!*" Swiftpaws added. "Give back the gold right now!"

"**GIVE BACK THE GOLD?!**" Tony roared. "Are you kidding? First I'll turn you back into **mini-mice**, and then I'll **CRUSH** you under my paws once and for all! One, Two, Three—what are you waiting for? **Get them!**"

Mini-Mice Versus Mega Tony!

At their boss's signal, the three **huge** bodyguards stomped toward us.

"**Supersuit: Tire mode!**" Swiftpaws exclaimed.

My superpartner quickly transformed into a big tire. Then he began to roll around the room. Once he'd gathered enough speed . . .

KABAAAAAM!

He hit One, Two, and Three full on!

"Get up, you lazy louses!" **SLICKFUR** yelled to the henchmice as he scurried toward the **DRILLMOBILE**.

"Where do you think you're going?" said

Lady Wonderwhiskers, using a series of **super-agile** acrobatic moves to block Slickfur's path.

"**Scram**, you supersnoop!" Tony Sludge's assistant screeched.

But before he could **escape**, Lady Wonderwhiskers whipped out a

ROPE and lassoed him. Soon Slickfur was all tied up.

"Get me out of here!" Slickfur yelled as he struggled to break free.

"Superstilton, you handle Tony!" Lady Wonderwhiskers hollered over her shoulder.

"*Me?!*" I exclaimed. "But how?"

"You'll **figure** it out," she shot back. "Remember: A Heromouse never gives up!"

Squeak! She was right, of course. So I **STRAIGHTENED** my tail and strode toward the boss of the Sewer Rats. "Pounds of provolone, stop right there, Tony!"

Those words activated my incredibly **cheesy** (but hard to predict) superpowers. A **HUGE** wheel of provolone cheese dropped from the ceiling and rolled right toward **Tony's** snout!

"Way to go, Superstilton!" rejoiced my

SUPERPOWER:
ROUND OF SPINNING PROVOLONE CHEESE
ACTIVATED WITH THE CRY:
"POUNDS OF PROVOLONE!"

superpartners.

But at the last minute, the boss of the **Sewer Rats** pointed the shrink ray at the cheese and **ZAP**!

The mega-wheel of provolone grew **smaller** and **smaller** until it was snack-sized. It bounced harmlessly off the tip of Tony's tail.

"Did you think you could foil me with this prank, you **SUPERZERO**?" He snickered.

"Umm . . . well, I . . ." I began.

"**Now you will pay!**" Tony roared. He pointed the shrink ray at me and . . .

ZAP!

I dodged the first ray.

ZAP!!

I dodged the second ray.

Zip!!!

The third ray hit me square on.

"Help!" I squeaked.

Gallons of Gorgonzola, I was shrinking again! Soon I'd be smaller than an **ant**!

"Come on, superpartner!" Swiftpaws said. "You need to **sneeze** again!"

"**But how?!**" I protested.

Tony lurched toward me. He picked me up in one enormouse **PAW** and squeezed me tight!

"I've got you right where I want you, cheddarface! Now I will crush you and squeeze you . . ."

At that moment, the smell of Tony's aftershave went RIGHT up my nose. It tickled my whiskers until suddenly . . .

"Aaachoo!"

I sneezed! In a split second, I'd returned to **normal** size, and I burst out of Tony's grip.

Tony jumped back in ASTONISHMENT. The shrink ray slipped from his paw, flew into the air, and then crashed to the ground, setting off **sparks** all over the place!

CRASH!

ZAP, ZAP, ZAP!

ZOOT!

"You cheesehead!" Tony exclaimed, bending down to pick it up. "Look what you've done!"

"**Uh-oh**, be careful, Boss!" Slickfur cried. "It could be dangerous!"

Too late. As soon as **Tony** touched the device . . .

ZAAAPP!

Tony was surrounded by a reddish glow. Then he began to **grow and grow and grow**!

The Final Supersneeze

In a matter of seconds, Tony was so huge, his ears grazed the ceiling!

"Whoa," he said. "You're a GENIUS, Slickfur!"

"T-thanks, Boss," his second-in-command stuttered, LOOKING UP at Tony in awe.

"And now, if you don't mind, I have a city to conquer!" Mega Tony declared.

He laughed triumphantly, and then pushed up the sewer grate and popped up right in the center of Swiss Square.

"We've got to stop him!" Lady Wonderwhiskers exclaimed.

"Uh, but how?" Swiftpaws asked in alarm.

"He's so huge, he's Mega Tony to the max!"

"We need to make him sneeze," I exclaimed. "Maybe the antidote works in reverse, too."

"Good idea," Lady Wonderwhiskers cheered. "Let's go!"

Swiftpaws transformed into a super flying scooter, and Lady Wonderwhiskers and I jumped on board.

VROOOOOOMM!

We zoomed out of the sewers.

Outside, the square was in total chaos.

Mega Tony

was causing MAYHEM everywhere.

"I will demolish the city if you don't obey my every command!" the Sewer Rat snickered. "Ha, ha, ha!"

He leaped forward until he reached Rat Tower, the tallest skyscraper in Muskrat City. Then he climbed to the TOP!

"Did you hear me?" he thundered. "Muskrat City is miiiine!"

"Forget it, Sludge!" Lady Wonderwhiskers exclaimed as we WHIZZED around his snout in our flying scooter.

"Catch us if you can, you supersized, supersmelly sewer rat!" Swiftpaws added.

"Shush your snouts, mini-mice!" he roared.

"Come on, Superstilton!" said Lady Wonderwhiskers. "Try to make him sneeze!"

"But how?!" I asked.

I had no idea how to do it, but I had to

Come here, mini-mice!

You supersized Sewer Rat!

try! So I stepped off the scooter and zoomed through the air like a true Heromouse.

"Good luck!" Swiftpaws yelled as he **whizzed** away, zipping right beneath Tony's nose.

But the mega sewer rat was too quick. With a ***lightning-fast*** move, he managed to pluck my friends out of midair.

"**Ha, ha, ha!** Freshly squeezed Heromice, coming right up!" Tony snickered.

"*Peppery Parmesan flakes, let them go right now!*" I cried.

Suddenly, a cloud of black pepper Parmesan flakes formed in front of Tony's enormouse snout.

"What's happening?!" he gasped as **crumbs** of peppery Parmesan **rained** down.

"**Aaaahhh!**" Tony shrieked. "My eyes

are watering, my nose is tickling, and my throat is itching . . . aaaa . . .

"Aaah-chooooo!"

It was a truly enormouse sneeze. Instantly, Tony got **SMALLER** and **SMALLER** and

SMALLER, until at last he was back to his usual size!

"**Noooooooo!**" he growled as he lost his grip on Rat Tower.

He fell down, down, down toward the street.

On the way, he bounced between laundry lines, slid down a gutter, and finally landed in an open sewer hole.

Splaaaaasssh!

"I'll get you for this, you supersnoops!" he howled.

Meanwhile, we tried to stop SLICKFUR and ONE, TWO, and THREE, but the Drillmobile was already speeding away.

"Supersonic Swiss slices, they're getting away!" Swiftpaws cried.

Tony and his crew had escaped again. There was nothing left to do but check to see if they'd taken the GOLD BARS with them. But luckily, the sparkly mountain was still in its place in the abandoned subway station.

"TOO BAD the shrink ray is broken now," Swiftpaws muttered, looking at the GOLD BARS.

"Why?" I asked.

"If we **shrank down** the gold, it'd be a lot easier to get it back to **RatCash Reserve**," he replied with a **WINK**.

All Because of a Load of Laundry

LUCKILY, the Muskrat City police stepped in and agreed to get the gold back where it belonged. A **CRANE** arrived at Swiss Square, fished up the loot, and loaded it on **ARMORED** trucks headed for RatCash Reserve.

Then Commissioner Ratford and Tess arrived, along with Proton and Electron.

"Slickfur's ***shrink ray*** was really tough to beat." Ratford sighed.

"But it wasn't totally foolproof," Tess replied. "As an invention, it's not even **sneeze**-proof! Ha, ha, ha!"

Lady Wonderwhiskers turned to me.

"We did it!" she said with one of her mouserific **smiles**.

"For sure," Swiftpaws replied. "And I really worked up an appetite. I'm hungrier than a rodent on a MouseFast diet!"

"You're in luck!" Tess said. "I just put a big tray of **cheese puffs** in the oven. Lady Wonderwhiskers, will you join us?"

My whiskers began to **tremble** in blissful anticipation. Would I get to sit next to her?

But then there was a flash of light, and Lady Wonderwhiskers was gone!

"W-where'd she go?" I stuttered, looking around in disappointment.

Great gobs of Gouda, once again that fascinating Heromouse had disappeared without a trace!

"You'll see her again soon, hero

partner," Swiftpaws said as we headed for **Heromice Headquarters**.

My only consolation was Tess's delicious meal, which awaited us at headquarters. And believe me, it was whisker-licking good!

Finally, it was time to go back home to

New Mouse City. I hugged my **HERO PALS** good-bye.

"See you next time, Superstilton," Tess said. "It won't be long. After all, Muskrat City will always need the Heromice!"

I smiled. Then I made a running start and took to the air.

Whoosh!

When I arrived back home, the sun was about to SET.

I hid in a deserted alley. Once I was sure no one was around, I activated my **Superpen**, and my supersuit disappeared.

I was about to scurry back to my mousehole when suddenly I remembered that my laundry was still in the machine back at the Wash-o-matic!

I rushed over, but once I was inside I had

to make my way through the crowd of chattering rodents.

What was going on?

"Ummm . . . excuse me," I said, sidling toward my washing machine.

"Sir, is that YOUR laundry?" one of the other customers asked me.

"Yes, why?" I asked.

"What do you mean, why?!" the customer replied. "You left it in there all day! By now it must have turned into a supersmoothie!"

"W-WHAT?!" I stammered.

I began to push all the buttons at random. At last, I managed to turn it off.

Then I pulled the HANDLE and . . .

"Stop!" the other customer cried.

Too late.

The door swung open with a clack!

An avalanche of suds spilled out of the washing machine and flooded the room.

BLUB, BLUB, BLUB!

Oh no! I had (again) broken a washing machine and had (again) flooded the place! What a CAT-ASTROPHE!

"Look, Mom!" cried a mouseling as he chased the floating soap bubbles.

When I pulled my sopping LAUNDRY out of the machine, I almost fainted. My clothes had shrunk!

They were all miniscule. In fact, they were practically microscopic!

Well, I had certainly had my fair share of shrinking for the day, so I saved my mini

Humpf!
What a disaster!
Ha, ha, ha!

clothes as a memento. I had a lot of good things to remember. After all, my latest **ADVENTURE** in Muskrat City had proved once more that

NOTHING IS IMPOSSIBLE FOR THE HEROMICE!

Be sure to read all my fabumouse adventures!

#1 Lost Treasure of the Emerald Eye

#2 The Curse of the Cheese Pyramid

#3 Cat and Mouse in a Haunted House

#4 I'm Too Fond of My Fur!

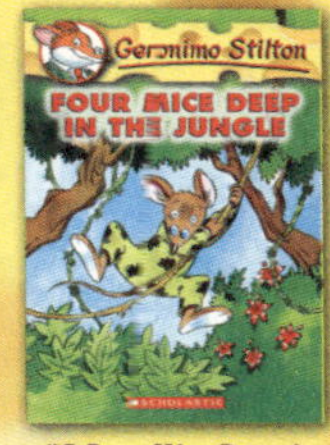

#5 Four Mice Deep in the Jungle

#6 Paws Off, Cheddarface!

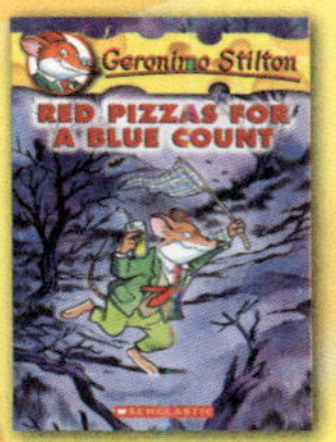

#7 Red Pizzas for a Blue Count

#8 Attack of the Bandit Cats

#9 A Fabumouse Vacation for Geronimo

#10 All Because of a Cup of Coffee

#11 It's Halloween, You 'Fraidy Mouse!

#12 Merry Christmas, Geronimo!

#13 The Phantom of the Subway

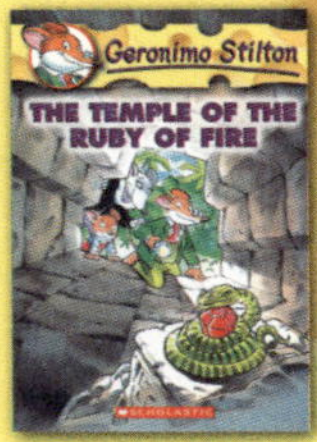

#14 The Temple of the Ruby of Fire

#15 The Mona Mousa Code

#16 A Cheese-Colored Camper

#17 Watch Your Whiskers, Stilton!

#18 Shipwreck on the Pirate Islands

#19 My Name Is Stilton, Geronimo Stilton

#20 Surf's Up, Geronimo!

#21 The Wild, Wild West

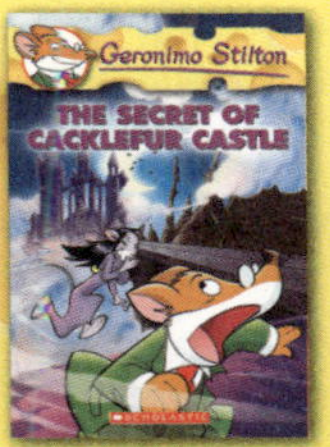

#22 The Secret of Cacklefur Castle

A Christmas Tale

#23 Valentine's Day Disaster

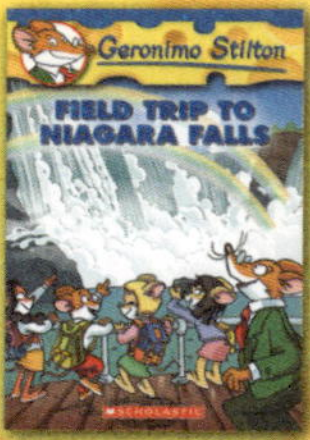

#24 Field Trip to Niagara Falls

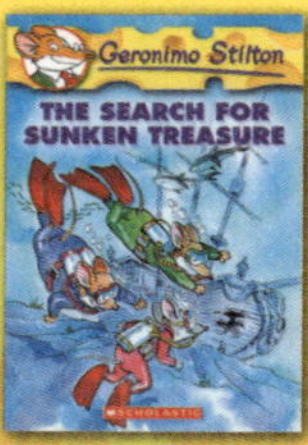

#25 The Search for Sunken Treasure

#26 The Mummy with No Name

#27 The Christmas Toy Factory

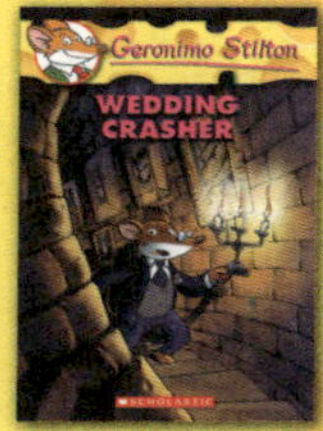

#28 Wedding Crasher

#29 Down and Out Down Under

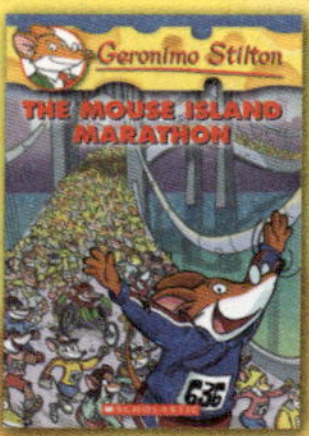

#30 The Mouse Island Marathon

#31 The Mysterious Cheese Thief

Christmas Catastrophe

#32 Valley of the Giant Skeletons

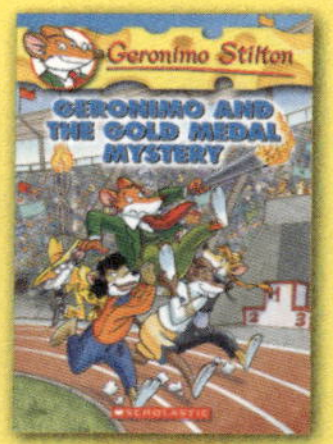

#33 Geronimo and the Gold Medal Mystery

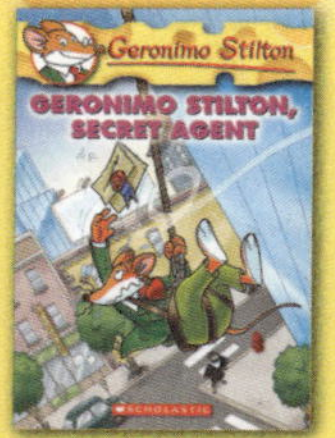

#34 Geronimo Stilton, Secret Agent

#35 A Very Merry Christmas

#36 Geronimo's Valentine

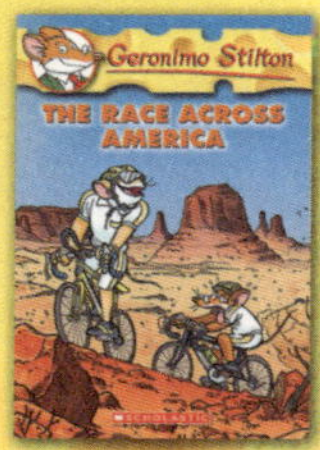

#37 The Race Across America

#38 A Fabumouse School Adventure

#39 Singing Sensation

#40 The Karate Mouse

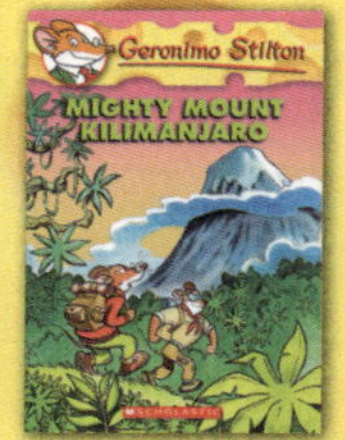

#41 Mighty Mount Kilimanjaro

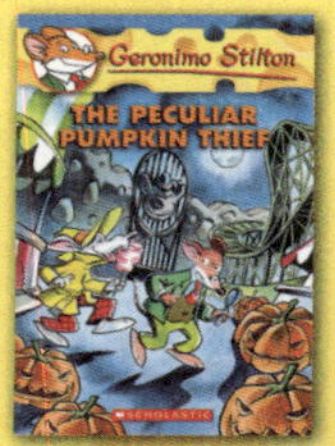

#42 The Peculiar Pumpkin Thief

#43 I'm Not a Supermouse!

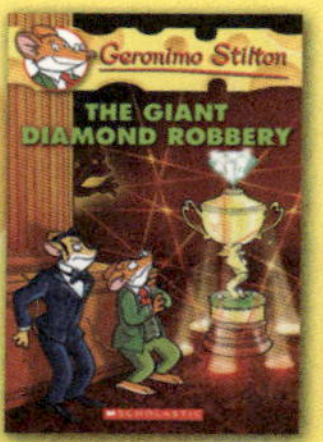

#44 The Giant Diamond Robbery

#45 Save the White Whale!

#46 The Haunted Castle

#47 Run for the Hills, Geronimo!

#48 The Mystery in Venice

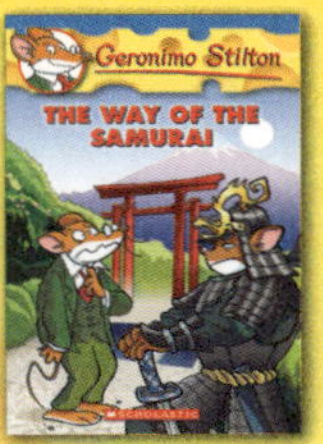

#49 The Way of the Samurai

#50 This Hotel Is Haunted!

#51 The Enormouse Pearl Heist

#52 Mouse in Space!

#53 Rumble in the Jungle

#54 Get into Gear, Stilton!

#55 The Golden Statue Plot

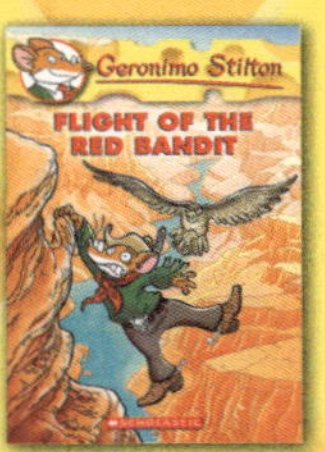

#56 Flight of the Red Bandit

#57 The Stinky Cheese Vacation

#58 The Super Chef Contest

#59 Welcome to Moldy Manor

#60 The Treasure of Easter Island

#61 Mouse House Hunter

#62 Mouse Overboard!

#63 The Cheese Experiment

#64 Magical Mission

#65 Bollywood Burglary

#66 Operation: Secret Recipe

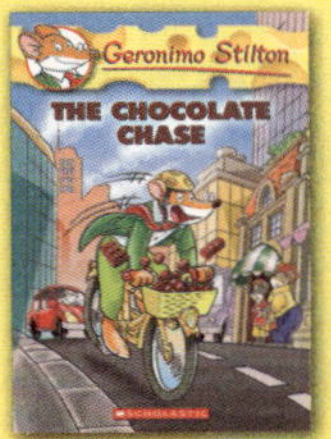

#67 The Chocolate Chase

#68 Cyber-Thief Showdown

DEAR MOUSE FRIENDS,
THANKS FOR READING, AND
FAREWELL TILL THE NEXT BOOK.
IT'LL BE ANOTHER
WHISKER-LICKING-GOOD
ADVENTURE, AND THAT'S
A PROMISE!